The Big Brown Box

By Marisabina Russo

Greenwillow Books, *An Imprint of HarperCollins Publishers*

For Ben,
Sam, and
Hannah

Gouache paints were used for the full-color art.
The text type is Futura Medium.

The Big Brown Box
Copyright © 2000 by Marisabina Russo Stark

Printed in Hong Kong by South China
Printing Company (1988) Ltd.
http://www.harperchildrens.com

Library of Congress
Cataloging-in-Publication Data

Russo, Marisabina.
The big brown box / by Marisabina Russo.
    p.   cm.
"Greenwillow Books."
Summary: As he plays in a very large box
in his room and turns it into a house, then
a cave, then a boat, Sam is reluctant to let
his little brother Ben join him, but then he
finds the perfect way for them to share.
ISBN 0-688-17096-X
[1. Boxes—Fiction.   2. Play—Fiction.
3. Sharing—Fiction.   4. Imagination—Fiction.
5. Brothers—Fiction.]   I. Title.   PZ7.R9192Bi
2000   [E]—dc21   99-14871   CIP

1 2 3 4 5 6 7 8 9 10   First Edition

The washing machine came in a big brown box.
Daddy was going to crush the box and fold it and
tie it with string and leave it for the recycling truck.

"Can I have the box, Daddy, please?" said Sam.

"It's so big. Where will you keep it?" said Daddy.

"In my room," said Sam.

"It will fill your whole room," said Daddy.

"I don't care," said Sam.

So Daddy carried the big brown box up the stairs
and squeezed it through the doorway into Sam's
room.
"What will you do with this box?" asked Daddy.
"I will make it my house with windows and a door.
I will park my truck outside on the rug," said Sam.

Sam drew the windows and door, and Mama
helped him cut them out.
Then Sam crawled in through the doorway.
He peeked out of one of the windows.

"Hi, Mama! Hi, Daddy!" said Sam.

Sam played in his new house until he heard
a *thump-thump-thump* on the wall.
"Who can that be?" said Sam.
He looked out the window. It was his brother, Ben.
"Go away!" said Sam.

"Me too!" said Ben.

"No! Go away, you monster baby. You are the big bad wolf," said Sam. "Leave my house alone!"

But Ben huffed and he puffed and tried to crawl in.

Sam pushed him back out.

Ben started to cry.

"What's the matter?" asked Mama as she walked
into the room.

"He's wrecking my house," said Sam.

"Me too," said Ben between sobs.

"Can't Ben come in for a visit?" asked Mama.
Sam said, "NO!"

"Please," said Ben.

"Please," said Mama. "Just for a few minutes."

"No, no, no," said Sam.

The next day Sam got tired of his
house. He turned the box on its
side and made it into a cave.
Then he heard a *thump-thump-thump*.
There was Ben, hitting the side of
the box.
"Go away!" said Sam.

"Me too," said Ben.
"You are a scary, hairy bear, and bears
don't belong in my cave," said Sam.

"Please!" screamed Ben until Daddy came in to see what
was wrong.
"You have lots of room," said Daddy. "Why don't you let Ben
come in?"
"Because he is a bear, and he'll wreck everything," said Sam.

The next day Sam got tired of his cave. He turned
the box over and made it into a boat. He went out
to sea.
When Sam was looking through his spyglass,
he heard a *thump-thump-thump*.
It was Ben banging on the box with his bottle.
"Go away!" said Sam.

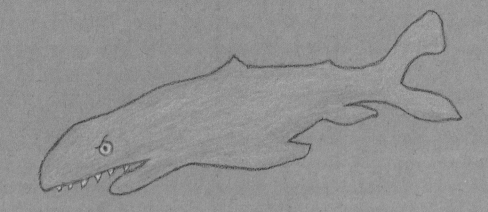

"You are a vicious silver shark, and you will eat me
if I let you in," said Sam.
Ben began to cry.
Mama came into Sam's room. She picked up Ben
and said, "Come on, Ben, I have something for you."

The next day Sam looked at the big brown box. "What shall I do today?" Sam wondered.
Then along came Ben. He was dragging a brown box behind him. It wasn't as big as Sam's, but it was just the right size for Ben.

Ben put his box next to Sam's.
"Me too," Ben said as he climbed into his box.
Now Sam was in the big brown box, and Ben
was in the little brown box.
Then Sam had an idea.

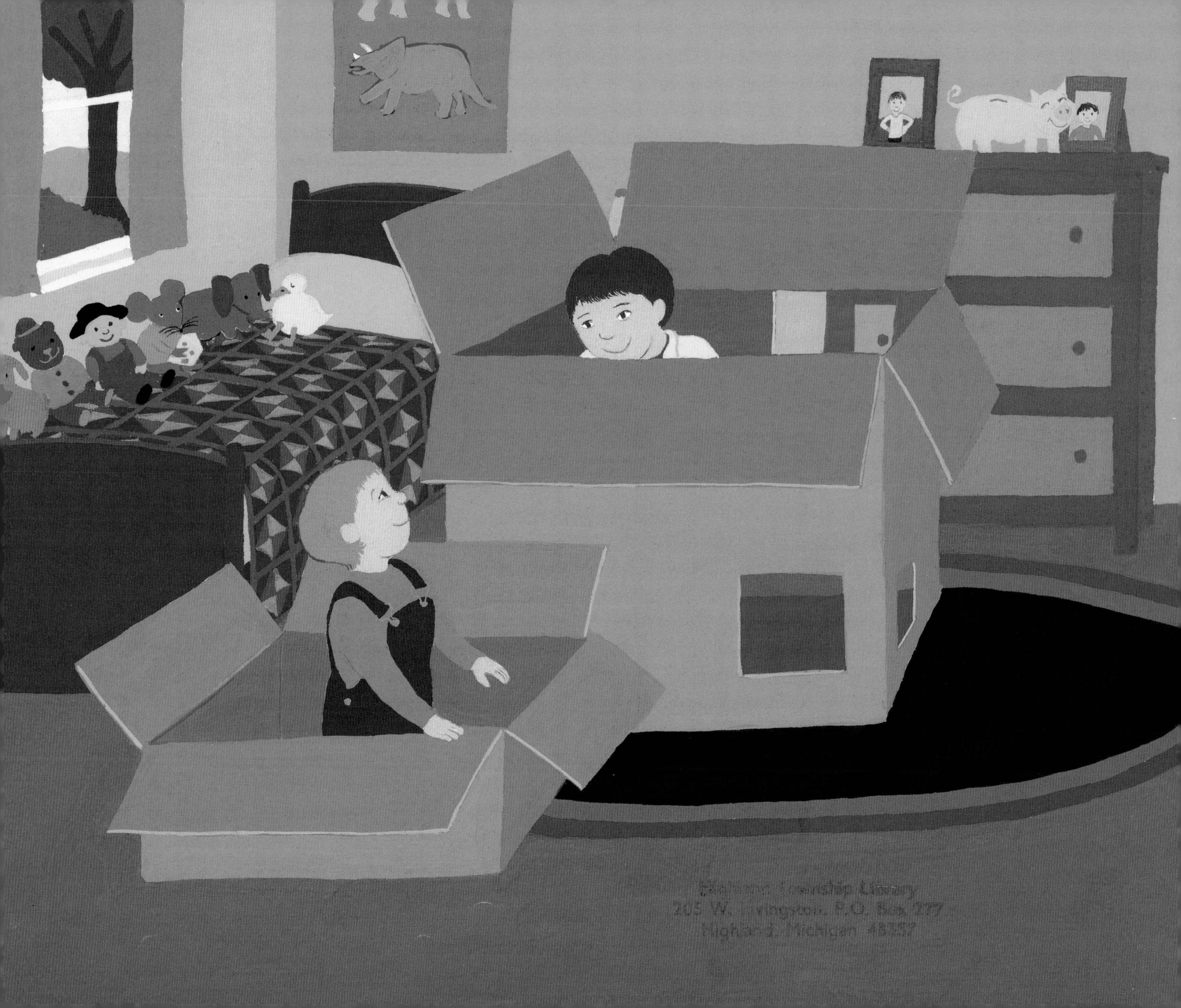

"Today we are in our spaceships, and we're
getting ready for blast off," said Sam.
He crouched down in his box.
Ben crouched down in his box too.
"Three, two, one . . . BLAST OFF!" yelled Sam.
"Two, one . . . OFF!" yelled Ben.

And off they went—Sam in the big brown box
and Ben in the little brown box—out into space,
up to the moon, and back to earth, where they
landed in Sam's room just in time for lunch.